Weekly Reader Books Presents

Buster Loves Buttons!

By
Fran Manushkin

Illustrated by
Dirk Zimmer

An I Can Read Book®

Harper & Row, Publishers

Buster Loves Buttons!
Text copyright © 1985 by Frances Manushkin
Illustrations copyright © 1985 by Dirk Zimmer
All rights reserved. No part of this book may be
used or reproduced in any manner whatsoever without
written permission except in the case of brief quotations
embodied in critical articles and reviews. Printed in
the United States of America. For information address
Harper & Row Junior Books, 10 East 53rd Street,
New York, N.Y. 10022. Published simultaneously in
Canada by Fitzhenry & Whiteside Limited, Toronto.
10 9 8 7 6 5 4 3 2 1
First Edition

Library of Congress Cataloging in Publication Data
Manushkin, Fran.
  Buster loves buttons!

  (An I can read book)
  Summary: After buying all the buttons he can, Buster,
the button glutton, begins stealing them off people's
clothes until Zippy and her dog decide to stop him.
    l. Children's stories, American. [l. Buttons—
Collectors and collecting—Fiction]   I. Zimmer, Dirk, ill.
II. Title.   III. Series.
PZ7.M3195Bus 1985   [E]   84-48332
ISBN 0-06-024107-1
ISBN 0-06-024108-X (lib. bdg.)

For Nina, a glutton for punishment

Buster loved buttons.

He had bottles of buttons

and baskets of buttons

and buckets and buckets of buttons.

Buster flew from town to town

in his big yellow plane

buying buttons.

10

He bought billions!

"Buttons are beautiful!"

said Buster.

He built one mountain

of red buttons

with two holes

and two mountains

of yellow buttons

with three holes

and three mountains

of all the rest.

13

Then he mixed them all up

and started over.

"Buttons are the best fun

in the world," said Buster.

He never went anywhere

without his bag of buttons.

15

But one day

there were no more buttons to buy.

Buster had bought them all.

16

"I must have more buttons!"

Buster cried.

So he bought a pair of scissors.

He sneaked up to a girl,

and *snip-snip-snip*,

Buster snipped her buttons!

18

"Phooey!" said the girl.

"Terrific!" yelled Buster.

"I got three green buttons

with four holes."

Buster put the buttons

in his big bag.

Then Buster leaped on a bus.

"Button, button,

who has your buttons?"

Buster asked.

And *snip-snip-snip,*

"I do!" Buster yelled.

"Everybody off the bus!"

called the driver.

"No buttons, no driving!"

Buster flew his yellow plane

to the circus.

He snipped the buttons

from the clowns

and made them cry.

Buster jumped up and down

on the big soft buttons.

"Clown buttons are bouncy!"

Buster laughed.

Buster hunted for buttons

everywhere.

He snipped buttons

from teddy bears,

25

buttons from party shoes,

buttons from overalls,

27

buttons from underwear,

buttons from EVERYWHERE.

One day

Buster sneaked up

on a dog named Sutton.

"Here, Sutton!" Buster called.

And *snip-snip-snip*,

Buster snipped Sutton's buttons.

"Glass buttons are the best!"

bragged Buster.

31

"Arf! Arf!" cried Sutton,

and he ran up to Kippy.

Kippy gave him a hug.

"Picking on *my* puppy

is the last straw," she said.

32

"I am going to catch

this button glutton."

33

Kippy ran home.

She sewed lots of glass buttons

on a big red bag.

"Oh, Buster!" called Kippy.

"How would you like

these shiny glass buttons?"

"I'd love them!" yelled Buster.

Buster leaped at the bag,

but Kippy raced down the street.

Buster ran after her.

Kippy and Sutton

took off in a plane.

Buster leaped onto his plane
and took off too.

Buster flew his plane

very close to Kippy.

"Give me those buttons!"

Buster roared.

"Here they are!"

shouted Kippy.

She waved the bag

of shiny glass buttons.

39

Buster covered his eyes.

"I can't see a thing!

Stop that!" Buster cried.

"I will stop

if you give me Sutton's buttons,"

said Kippy.

"Never!" yelled Buster.

Kippy flew her plane

over the sea.

Buster flew right behind her.

Kippy flew her plane

upside down.

Buster flew *his* plane

upside down.

"Oh no!" cried Buster.

"I'm losing my buttons!"

"Alley-oooop!" sang Kippy,

and *PLOP!—*

she caught Buster's buttons.

"Give me back my buttons!"

cried Buster.

"No!" said Kippy.

"They belong to my friends.

Now pull the rope, Sutton!"

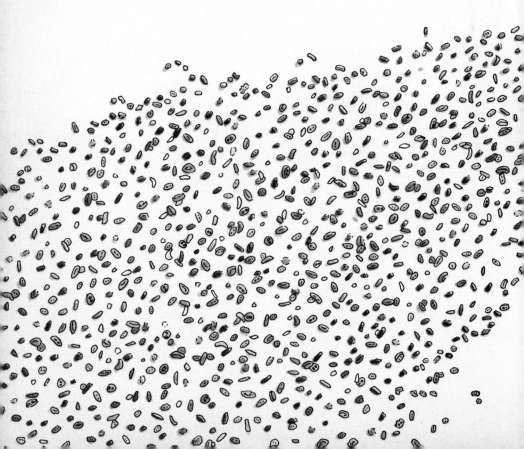

Sutton pulled and pulled.

BILLIONS OF BUTTONS

rained down on the town.

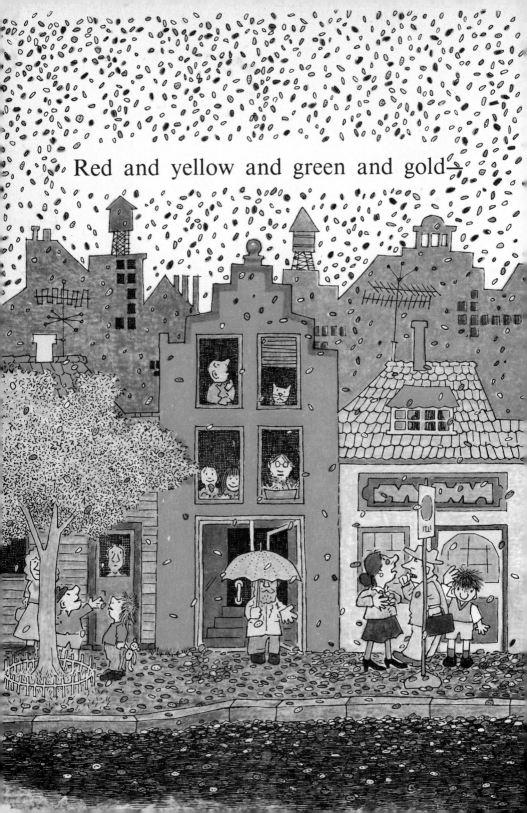

Red and yellow and green and gold—

A sky full of beautiful buttons!

The happy clown

caught buttons

in his spoon.

The bus driver

caught buttons in his hat.

And the little girl

caught buttons

in her baseball glove.

50

"Oh, no," cried Buster.

"I have lost

all my beautiful buttons."

When Kippy landed,

everyone cheered.

52

When Buster landed,

they booed.

"Bad button glutton,"

said the girl.

"You are going to jail, Buster,"

said the bus driver.

54

"Arf!" barked Sutton.

"Are there buttons in jail?"

asked Buster.

"There are buttons everywhere,"

said the clown.

56

"It will take years

to sort them out."

57

"I will sort them,"

shouted Buster.

"Arf!" Sutton barked.

"Will you find

Sutton's buttons first?"

asked Kippy.

"Yes, I will," promised Buster.

Buster started sorting buttons
right away.

And everyone in town was
happy again.

But Buster the button glutton

was the happiest of all.

THE END